Let's Roll
SPORTS CARS

by Wendy Hinote Lanier

FOCUS READERS

www.northstareditions.com

Copyright © 2017 by North Star Editions, Lake Elmo, MN 55042. All rights reserved. No part of this book may be reproduced or utilized in any form or by any means without written permission from the publisher.

Produced for North Star Editions by Red Line Editorial.

Photographs ©: Gustavo Fadel/Shutterstock Images, cover, 1; Darren Brode/Shutterstock Images, 4–5, 19; John_Silver/Shutterstock Images, 6; AP Images, 8–9; LagunaticPhoto/Shutterstock Images, 10; allanw/Shutterstock Images, 13; Maxal Tamor/Shutterstock Images, 14–15; ermess/Shutterstock Images, 16; Dong liu/Shutterstock Images, 20–21, 29; Jordan Tan/Shutterstock Images, 23; Gene Blevins/LA DailyNews/ZumaPress/AP Images, 24; Fingerhut/Shutterstock Images, 26–27

ISBN
978-1-63517-050-4 (hardcover)
978-1-63517-106-8 (paperback)
978-1-63517-207-2 (ebook pdf)
978-1-63517-157-0 (hosted ebook)

Library of Congress Control Number: 2016913841

Printed in the United States of America
Mankato, MN
November, 2016

About the Author

Wendy Hinote Lanier is a native Texan and former elementary teacher who writes and speaks to children and adults on a variety of topics. She is the author of more than 20 books for children and young people. Some of her favorite people are dogs.

TABLE OF CONTENTS

CHAPTER 1
One Fabulous Week 5

CHAPTER 2
Sports Car History 9

CHAPTER 3
What Makes a Sports Car? 15

CHAPTER 4
Sports Cars of Today 21

More Power! 26

Focus on Sports Cars • 28
Glossary • 30
To Learn More • 31
Index • 32

CHAPTER 1

ONE FABULOUS WEEK

Monterey Car Week is an entire week devoted to car shows, auctions, and races. On opening night, sports car enthusiasts line the streets. They are excited to watch the Kickoff Cruise-In.

 **Lamborghinis are known for their doors that open upward rather than outward.**

 **The Ferrari 250 LM was produced in Italy between 1963 and 1965.**

In this event, hundreds of new and beautifully restored sports cars are on display.

The biggest event of the week is the races. Crowds gather at the famous Mazda Raceway to watch their favorite **vintage** cars in action. They cheer as the cars navigate the tight curves of the Laguna Seca corkscrew. Hundreds of classic cars take part.

AUCTIONS

The auctions during Monterey Car Week feature some of the most expensive cars in the world. In 2015, a private collection of 25 sports cars went to auction. At the final hammer, the cars sold for more than $75 million.

CHAPTER 2

SPORTS CAR HISTORY

The first automobiles appeared in the late 1800s. In the 1910s, Henry Ford started using an **assembly line** to produce his cars. This process made cars less expensive.

A driver takes part in a race in 1930.

 The Mercer Raceabout could reach speeds of 90 miles per hour (145 km/h).

Soon, many people who wanted a car could afford one. As cars became more common, racing became a popular new sport.

But racing called for powerful cars that could perform well. The first racing cars were really the first sports cars.

▸ EARLY SPORTS CARS

The Mercer Raceabout and the Stutz Bearcat were among the first American sports cars. The Mercer Raceabout was built from 1911 to 1915. The Stutz Bearcat was built between 1915 and 1922. Both cars were light and had powerful engines. They were composed of little more than an engine and a gas tank on a **chassis**.

During World War II (1939–1945), many American soldiers fought in Europe. While they were there, they started to appreciate European sports cars. European sports cars were built for hilly, winding roads. These cars used less fuel and had strong brakes.

The Morgan is a classic British sports car that has been built the same way since the 1930s.

 All Morgan cars are built by hand.

American soldiers found them fun to drive. The soldiers returned to the United States after the war. They created a demand for cars like the ones they had driven in Europe.

CHAPTER 3

WHAT MAKES A SPORTS CAR?

A sports car is typically a two-seat, two-door car with rear-wheel drive. It has a **responsive** engine that handles well on all types of roads. It rides low and is usually fast. But most of all, it's fun to drive.

 **Sports cars handle well around tight curves.**

 **Two Ferraris cruise the roads of Italy.**

Some sports cars are designed to race. Others are designed for the average driver to take on the

16

highway. Most sports cars are not practical for everyday use because of their small size. For most buyers, sports cars are a **luxury**.

SPORTS CAR CLUB

The Sports Car Club of America (SCCA) is a club for people who love sports cars. It began in 1944, and today it has more than 60,000 members. The SCCA oversees professional and club races, **road rallies**, and **autocross** events. Its members serve as race officials and workers for most professional races in the United States. Members also participate in SCCA-sponsored **amateur** events.

Companies that make sports cars race their cars. These companies know that racing is the best way to advertise their cars. A car that wins a race is likely to have higher sales. Some of the most popular race cars were developed by sports car companies such as Jaguar,

FUN FACT

The Mazda MX-5 is the best-selling two-seat convertible sports car of all time.

PARTS OF A SPORTS CAR

- two seats
- two-door design
- low to the ground

Lotus, and Ferrari. Disc brakes, a low-slung frame, and supercharged engines are examples of features that came out of race car designs.

CHAPTER 4

SPORTS CARS OF TODAY

Today there are many types of sports cars on the market. At the top of the market are the super cars. Super cars are fast and very expensive. They cost between $1.3 million and $4.8 million.

 **The McLaren P1 costs approximately $1.3 million, but many owners add extra features that push the price even higher.**

Super cars are usually produced in limited numbers. For instance, carmaker Aston Martin said it would produce only 99 of its AM-RB 001 model. Other examples of super cars include the Jaguar XJ220, the Bugatti Veyron, and the McLaren P1.

But super cars are only a small part of the sports car market. Entry-level cars are much less expensive. They include the Mazda MX-5 and the Subaru BRZ.

 More than one million Mazda MX-5s have been sold around the world.

Boxing star Floyd Mayweather Jr. bought a Koenigsegg CCXR Trevita in 2015.

Prices of entry-level sports cars start at approximately $25,000. Midlevel sports cars include the BMW Z4, the Porsche Boxster, and the Chevy Corvette. These cars start at approximately $50,000.

Sports cars may be a luxury that few can afford. But most people agree that it's thrilling to watch a sports car in action!

As of 2016, the most expensive sports car in the world is the Koenigsegg CCXR Trevita. Only three have ever been made, and the price is $4.85 million.

25

HOW IT WORKS

MORE POWER!

Some sports cars use superchargers or turbochargers to boost power. They pump pressurized air into the engine's cylinders. Superchargers are driven by a belt on the engine. Turbochargers are powered by the engine's exhaust. The added air allows more complete burning of fuel. This can result in better **mileage** and higher speeds.

The Ferrari V12 engine has won awards for its performance.

FOCUS ON
SPORTS CARS

Write your answers on a separate piece of paper.

1. Write a sentence that summarizes Chapter 2 of this book.
2. Would you want to attend Monterey Car Week? Why or why not?
3. Which of these is a midlevel sports car?
    - **A.** Porsche Boxster
    - **B.** Mazda MX-5
    - **C.** McLaren P1
4. Why was racing less common before the 1910s?
    - **A.** because assembly lines did not work well
    - **B.** because cars had not been invented yet
    - **C.** because most people could not afford cars

5. What does **enthusiasts** mean in this book?
- **A.** something that has been restored
- **B.** people who enjoy something
- **C.** things that line a street

On opening night, sports car **enthusiasts** line the streets. They are excited to watch the Kickoff Cruise-In.

6. What does **practical** mean in this book?
- **A.** useful
- **B.** big enough
- **C.** expensive

Most sports cars are not **practical** for everyday use because of their small size. For most buyers, sports cars are a luxury.

Answer key on page 32.

29

GLOSSARY

amateur
A person involved in an activity for enjoyment rather than money.

assembly line
A series of stations organized in a line to put together the parts of a whole product.

autocross
A sport that uses traffic cones to make a small racecourse.

chassis
The frame of a motor vehicle.

luxury
Something that is nice to have but not necessary.

mileage
The number of miles a vehicle can travel on a gallon of fuel.

responsive
Able to react quickly.

road rallies
A sport in which two-person teams drive cars over public roads.

vintage
Old but still in good condition.

TO LEARN MORE

BOOKS

Hamilton, John. *Sports Cars*. Minneapolis: Abdo Publishing, 2013.

Monnig, Alex. *Behind the Wheel of a Sports Car*. Mankato, MN: The Child's World, 2016.

Willson, Quentin. *Cool Cars*. New York: DK Publishing, 2014.

NOTE TO EDUCATORS

Visit **www.focusreaders.com** to find lesson plans, activities, links, and other resources related to this title.

INDEX

A
auctions, 5, 7

C
Chevy Corvette, 25

E
engines, 11, 15, 19, 26
entry-level cars, 22, 24

F
Ford, Henry, 9

K
Kickoff Cruise-In, 5

L
Laguna Seca, 7

M
Mazda MX-5, 22
Mazda Raceway, 7
McLaren P1, 22
midlevel cars, 24
Monterey Car Week, 5, 7

P
Porsche Boxster, 24

R
races, 5–6, 10–11, 16, 17, 18

S
Sports Car Club of America, 17
super cars, 21–22

W
World War II, 12

Answer Key: 1. Answers will vary; 2. Answers will vary; 3. A; 4. C; 5. B; 6. A

629.228 L   FLT
Lanier, Wendy Hinote,
Sports cars /

06/17